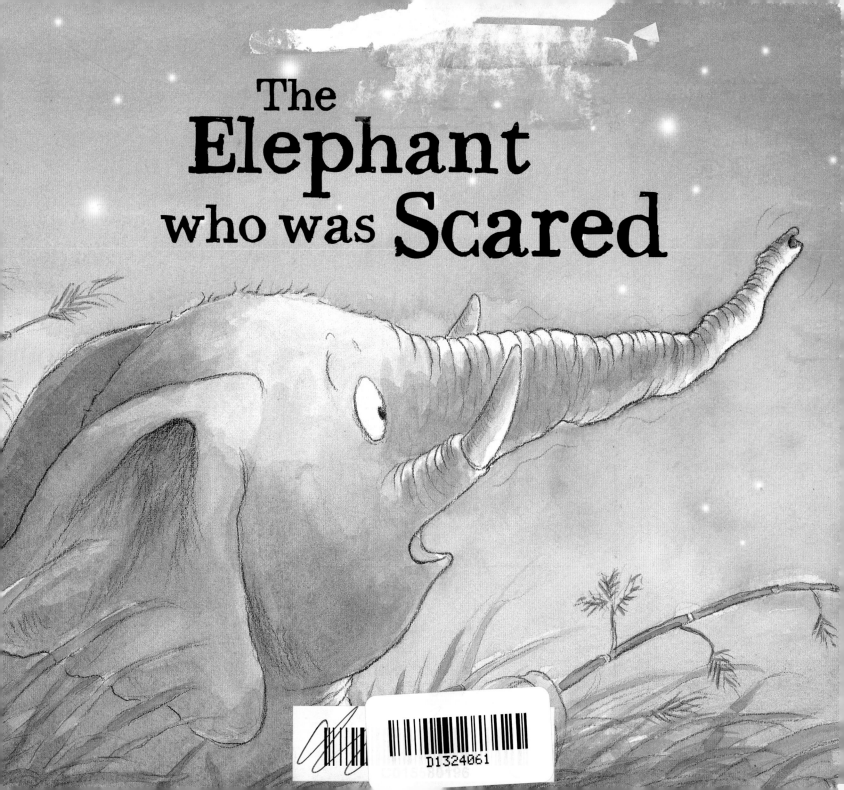

The Elephant
who was Scared

Designer: Fiona Hajée

Consultant: Cecilia A. Essau, Professor
of Developmental Psychopathology at
Roehampton University

Copyright © QED Publishing 2012

First published in the UK in 2012 by
QED Publishing
A Quarto Group Company
230 City Road
London EC1V 2TT

www.qed-publishing.co.uk

A catalogue record for this book is available from the British Library.

ISBN 978 1 84835 890 4

Printed in China

The Elephant who was Scared

Rachel Elliot

John Bendall-Brunello

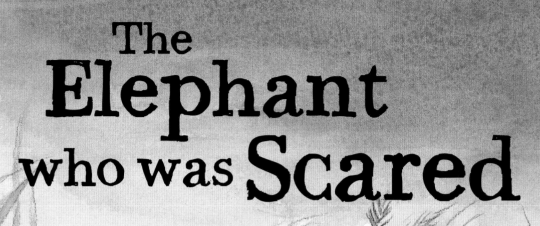

QED Publishing

Little Elephant was exploring.
At first it was exciting...

... but then he couldn't
find Mummy anywhere.

Suddenly the jungle seemed
very big and very very dark.

"Mummy?" he called.

No one replied.
Little Elephant was lost!

Poor Little Elephant felt very scared.
He didn't know where he was
and he didn't know the way home.

"I just want my mummy," cried Little Elephant.
Big tears rolled down his cheeks
and plopped onto the ground.

Then he heard a scary noise.

"EEK! SCREEK!"

"Help!"
whimpered
Little Elephant.

He tried to hide inside the long grasses, but he was too big.

"EEK! SCREEK!"

The noise was getting closer!

Little Elephant looked up.
"Wh-**who** are y-**you**?" he asked.

"Eek! I'm Fruit Bat,"
said the creature in the sky.

Little Elephant smiled.
He felt a bit better.

"I'm Little Elephant," he said. "I'm lost."

"Follow the stars," said Fruit Bat.
"The stars will guide you home."

Little Elephant looked at the bright stars
twinkling in the dark sky.

Little Elephant didn't feel so alone anymore.
But then he spotted two **big** scary eyes staring at him.

"I'm lost,"
said Little Elephant.
"Can you help me?"

"I'm Bushbaby,"
said a kind voice
from the tree.

"Follow that path,"
said Bushbaby, pointing.

"The stars
will light the way."

Little Elephant ran down the path.

But then he heard
a scary noise coming
from the bushes.

"WAAH! WAAH!"

Little Elephant's knees
knocked together!

Then he thought about Fruit Bat,
and Bushbaby and the stars.

He took a deep, brave breath.

"Hello," he said.
"I'm Little Elephant. Who are you?"

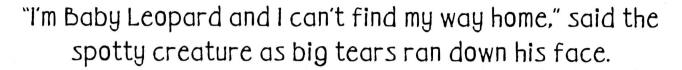

"I'm Baby Leopard and I can't find my way home," said the spotty creature as big tears ran down his face.

"I'm lost too," said Little Elephant. "Let's follow the stars together so we don't feel scared."

Baby Leopard gave a shy smile.
"Let's run!" she said.

Little Elephant
and Baby Leopard
ran side by side.

They charged
through the jungle.

Their feet drummed on the ground.
Louder and **louder!**
Faster and **faster!**

"This is FUN!"
shouted Little Elephant.

At last they reached Little Elephant's home.
Baby Leopard lived just around the corner.

Little Elephant told Mummy all
about his adventures:

"Fruit Bat and Bushbaby looked scary
but they were kind, and Baby Leopard
was scared — just like me.

But I'm not scared anymore!"

Mummy gave Little
Elephant a big cuddle.

The stars watched
over them as they both
fell fast asleep.

Next steps

- Ask your child how Little Elephant was feeling throughout the story, and why.

- Ask your child to try and remember the names of all the animals in the book; Little Elephant, Fruit Bat, Bushbaby and Baby Leopard. Has your child ever seen any of these types of animals?

- Discuss all the things that Little Elephant did to find his mother.

- Ask your child what they can see in the sky at night. Ask them to imagine some bright stars during a clear night and then suggest that they draw some stars using bright colours.

- Ask your child how they think Little Elephant felt when his mother gave him a big cuddle. How do they feel when they get a cuddle from someone who loves and cares for them?

Dealing with fear

If children feel scared, they should be encouraged to:

- ask for help from adults (e.g. teachers, parents, brothers and sisters) and their friends

- relax by taking deep breaths

- use positive statements, such as "I am brave". A good example of a positive statement from the story is when Little Elephant says, "Let's follow the stars together so we don't feel scared".

- try making a new friend or helping other people, just as Little Elephant did with Baby Leopard

- distract themselves from the scary situation by thinking of something that makes them happy. For example, thinking about the stars and the friendly bat and bushbaby made Little Elephant feel more confident; and running made Little Elephant and Baby Leopard feel happier.